AXEL STORM
DEATH VALLEY

For my wonderful designer, Thy

ORCHARD BOOKS
338 Euston Road, London NW1 3BH
Orchard Books Australia
Level 17/207 Kent Street, Sydney, NSW 2000

First published in 2010
First paperback publication in 2011

ISBN 978 1 40830 260 6 (hardback)
ISBN 978 1 40830 268 2 (paperback)

A CIP catalogue record for this book is available from the British Library.

1 3 5 7 9 10 8 6 4 2 (hardback)
1 3 5 7 9 10 8 6 4 2 (paperback)

Printed in Great Britain

Orchard Books is a division of Hachette Children's Books, an Hachette UK company.

DEATH VALLEY

SHOO RAYNER

CHAPTER ONE

"This is the slowest, most stupid horse in the whole world," Axel Storm grumbled. "I think he must be about one hundred and three years old!"

Mum, Dad and Axel were trekking along the scenic trail inside the security fence around their massive ranch.

Axel's mum and dad were rock stars. Their band, Stormy Skies, had recorded twenty-two platinum-selling hits in eighty-three different countries around the world. They spent half their lives travelling, performing concerts and meeting their millions of fans.

The Storms had come to Death Valley to perform at the Red Rock Festival, held in a giant open-air arena. They had hired a luxury cowboy ranch nearby for a couple of weeks.

"I'm sure they'll have better horses at the Celebrity Kids' Club Cowboy Ranch," Mum said sweetly.

"Oh, *please* don't make me go there!" Axel whined. "They only have Shetland ponies because they're scared that a famous kid might fall off a big horse and hurt themselves. My feet touch the ground when I sit on one!"

"Well, we can't look after you during the festival," Dad explained. "There will be photographers everywhere. We want you to grow up like a normal boy. You can't be normal if you're in the newspapers all the time."

"Oh, b-but...!" Axel stammered. "The Celebrity Kids' Club Cowboy Ranch is *so-o-o* boring. All I did last time was learn to lasso and get my rope-handling certificate."

Just then, they heard an extraordinary noise in the distance. It sounded like a herd of mooing cows!

MOO!

Far across the plain, a streak of grey dust zoomed towards them. As it came closer, the sound grew louder.

But it wasn't cows – the noise was coming from the sound system of an enormous Sports Utility Vehicle which was speeding across the wide open grasslands. Gigantic cow horns stretched across the front of its bonnet.

"Oh no! It's your Uncle Ritchie," said Dad. "He always liked things loud and fast. I thought he was away on business."

The car drove right up to them, slammed on the brakes, skidded to a stop, and disappeared in a cloud of dust.

As the dust settled, a huge man got out of the car and stood silhouetted against the sun. He walked towards them and ruffled Axel's hair.

"Hey, Axel!" he bellowed. "Long time, no see, kid! My, you sure have grown!"

Axel sighed. Why did grown-ups always say that?

Uncle Ritchie grabbed Dad in a bear hug. "Why didn't you come and stay with me on my ranch, little brother?" he boomed. "There's plenty of room for you all, and it's only just across the valley."

Uncle Ritchie was even richer than Mum and Dad. He'd made a fortune in the oil business. His ranch was enormous.

"This suits us fine for the festival," Mum squeaked, as Uncle Ritchie nearly squeezed the life out of her in a hug.

"This is just a ranch for people who wanna play cowboys," Uncle Ritchie huffed. "These horses should'a been retired years ago."

"That's what I said," Axel chipped in. "And tomorrow I've got to go to the Celebrity Kids' Club Cowboy Ranch and ride their stupid tiny ponies!"

"The heck you are!" Uncle Ritchie thundered. "No nephew of mine is going to play at cowboys when I've got a herd of cattle needin' to be rounded up. You'll come with me and be a *real* cowboy."

"Wow! That sounds great," Axel grinned. "I can use my rope-handling skills!"

"It sounds a bit dangerous." Mum looked worried.

"We want to keep Axel away from photographers, especially that horrible Archie Flash from *Celebrity Gossip Magazine*," said Dad.

Uncle Ritchie pulled a lasso out of the car and whirled it round his head. "Anyone poking their cameras where they ain't wanted is gonna get caught!" he sneered.

"OK!" Dad sighed. He knew that Uncle Ritchie would get his way in the end.

"See you tomorrow!" Uncle Ritchie yelled, as he spun the wheels on his truck and disappeared into the distance.

"*Yee-hah!*" Axel cheered, hurling his hat into the air.

CHAPTER TWO

Uncle Ritchie threw a coil of rope at Axel. “Let’s see these rope-handlin’ skills of yours, son,” he boomed.

Reluctantly, Mum and Dad had dropped Axel off at Uncle Ritchie’s ranch on their way to the concert rehearsals. Uncle Ritchie was taking Axel on an expedition into the Red Rock Mountains to round up his cattle and bring them home for the winter.

Uncle Ritchie's ranch was enormous. All around the house were paddocks and stables for his hundreds of horses.

Axel tried to remember his lasso lessons. He twisted coils of rope into his left hand and made a loop in his right. He flipped the loop over his wrist and slowly twirled the rope around his head. He'd practised a lot at the Celebrity Kids' Club Ranch last year. The flowing movement came back to him in no time.

He fixed his aim on a fencepost and hurled the loop towards it.

As the slipknot hit the post, Axel pulled his right arm back and the knot pulled tight.

"Wheeww!" Uncle Ritchie whistled. "You sure are good!"

"Wayne Laramie, the cowboy film star, gave me extra lessons at a boring film premiere party," Axel explained.

"Well, I hope he showed you how to ride a real horse, too!" Uncle Ritchie walked off towards the paddocks. "Come and choose one for yourself."

Uncle Ritchie leant against the fence. Axel climbed up and sat on the top. Four beautiful palomino horses trotted together around the paddock.

"Take your pick," Uncle Ritchie said, with a twinkle in his eye.

Axel studied them carefully. He'd been given his first pony when he was just a toddler, so he knew a little bit about horses.

One of the horses stood out from the others. Axel didn't know why. It was just a feeling – he sensed some kind of bond with it.

He pointed across the paddock. "That one."

"Wheeew!" Uncle Ritchie whistled again. "Good choice – if you're brave enough! You'd better go and show him who's boss!" Uncle Ritchie winked and smiled, but he gave Axel no clue what to do.

Axel slipped off the fence and slowly walked across the paddock towards the horses. He felt very alone, like a batsman walking to the crease, or a striker preparing for a penalty shot.

The other horses skittered away. But his horse stood its ground. It snorted and turned its head away, ignoring Axel as if he were nothing more than a frisky young colt.

Axel did the same. He never once looked the horse in the eye. Slowly and patiently, whispering calming words, he sidled across the paddock, until he was standing next to the magnificent animal.

He could feel the heat of its body and breathed in its grassy, summer-meadow smell. He stood like that for what seemed like for ever – waiting for a sign.

Then the horse whinnied, bowed and turned its head towards him. Axel felt a smile creep over his face. He put his hand up and gently touched the horse's neck. They were connected. Somehow, Axel knew the horse had accepted him.

Axel turned and walked back to his uncle. He didn't look round. He knew the horse would follow him.

"Wow!" Uncle Ritchie exclaimed. "You sure have a way with horses. What are you gonna call him?"

Axel turned and stroked the horse on the forehead. "I'll call him...Hurricane!"

The horse neighed his approval.

Soon Axel was sitting high up on Hurricane, riding alongside his uncle on a tour of the ranch. He felt as though he'd ridden Hurricane for years. They were made for each other.

The sun slowly dipped below the mountains. The peaks glowed red, as if they were on fire.

"We'd better get these horses fed and watered," said Uncle Ritchie. "We've got an early start tomorrow."

Axel couldn't wait!

CHAPTER THREE

The next morning, high up on the mountainside, Axel had a fantastic view of Death Valley. The Red Rock Festival had started and the faint sounds of music drifted up to him. There were tents and camper vans everywhere, with hundreds of people milling around the food stalls and stages.

All around him cattle mooed in the high meadows, happily chewing the last of the summer grass. The air was crisp and fresh. It felt like winter wasn't too far away. It was time to get the cattle safely rounded up before the first snow fell.

"Here's what we're gonna do," said Uncle Ritchie. "We're gonna ride up to the top meadows with the other men, and work our way down, collecting up cattle as we go. When we're ready, we'll drive them across Death Valley and back home to the ranch."

"Let's go!" Axel cheered.

As the small team of cowboys rode up the mountain track, Uncle Ritchie told Axel about the cattle. "They like to move together in a herd," he explained. "If we can find the bull leader and get him to come along with us, the rest will follow."

Eventually the grass gave way to rocky gravel. Lonely pine trees were the only green to be seen. An eagle floated on the breeze above them.

Uncle Ritchie raised his hand and whistled loudly through his teeth – a signal to the others. The cattle drive had begun! There'd be no rest until the cattle were all safely penned up in the ranch at home.

The cowboys spread out, whooping, whistling and shouting instructions to each other.

Axel and his uncle turned their horses round and started the downhill descent. Hurricane was fast and sure-footed. Axel felt like he was at one with the horse.

They began driving the cattle down the mountainside towards a hollow canyon that acted like a natural pen. There they would collect the cattle up before they ventured out across Death Valley.

The noise was incredible. The cattle mooed loudly, protesting at being moved away from their summer home. Their hooves clattered and rumbled across the rocky terrain.

Axel helped Uncle Ritchie block the canyon, while the cowboy crew brought in the rest of the herd.

Soon the canyon was filled with a sea of restless cattle. The rocky walls echoed with their braying, and the ground quaked and shook with the trampling of thousands of hooves.

"Can you see him?" Uncle Ritchie asked.

"Who?" said Axel.

"The leader."

Axel screwed up his eyes and examined the teeming herd of cows. There were so many of them – and they all looked the same.

"Yes!" said Axel suddenly, pointing at a huge bull.

It was darker and bigger than the others. It had a white, clover-shaped pattern on its forehead.

"The others seem to follow him," Axel explained. "He looks like he's in charge."

"You're learning fast!" Uncle Ritchie smiled. "We'll make a cowboy of you yet!"

CHAPTER FOUR

"Follow me." Uncle Ritchie rode forwards, into the herd. "Take it slow, be careful and don't let them think you're afraid."

Axel followed, gently nudging Hurricane into the sea of heads that bobbed and twisted like waves, being careful not to get caught on any of the vicious-looking horns.

They worked their way round behind the lead bull, and gently nudged him towards the open mouth of the canyon.

Slowly, the huge beast made his way towards the exit. Obediently, the herd followed along in his trail. The cowboys waited outside the canyon, ready to guide the cattle towards Death Valley and home.

“We need to keep the lead bull nice and calm,” Uncle Ritchie said. “If he gets spooked, he’ll start to run away. All the rest will follow and before you know it, we’ll have a stampede on our hands. That would not be good.”

Axel positioned himself beside the bull’s left flank. They ambled out of the canyon, letting the mighty creature set a nice, gentle walking pace. Death Valley lay in front of them. It would take most of the afternoon to cross the hot, dusty plain.

Suddenly, a man lurched towards them on a tired, old horse. It was obvious that he'd never learnt to ride. The man pointed a camera at Axel and shouted, "Say cheese!"

"Archie Flash!" Axel hissed. "Go away! You'll frighten the cattle!"

Archie Flash worked for *Celebrity Gossip Magazine*. He would do anything to get a story about Axel.

"When you didn't arrive at the Celebrity Kids' Club Cowboy Ranch, I knew you must be doing something more exciting. I was right. Axel the Cowboy!" Archie cheered. "What a great story!"

Zap! Archie's powerful flashgun burst in a dazzle of bright light.

"You idiot!" Uncle Ritchie yelled.

It was too late. The lead bull went mad. It rolled its eyes and bellowed loudly. It pawed at the ground, snorted and charged at Archie. The rest of the herd blindly followed him – a thousand cattle running helter-skelter after their leader. The sound was deafening. The dust was blinding.

Axel blinked and took up the chase.

"STAMPEDE!" Uncle Ritchie hollered at the top of his voice.

CHAPTER FIVE

When Archie Flash's horse saw the wall of cows bearing down on them, it turned and ran for its life. Archie had no idea how to make it do anything else.

Axel saw the big bull charge up behind him and ram Archie's horse. The horse reared up high, Archie flew through the air...and landed right between the bull's massive horns!

Archie caught one of the horns and held onto it like a crazy rodeo rider. Having someone on its back made the bull even angrier. It ran faster, bucking and kicking, trying to hurl Archie off his back.

With every kick and bump, Archie's camera flashed and took a photograph. The flashes made the beast madder and madder.

Axel dug his heels into Hurricane's sides and urged him on. The Red Rock Festival entrance was getting closer and closer. He could hear the sounds of his mum and dad singing.

If we don't stop this stampede soon, Axel thought, *people are going to die!*

All around him the cattle bellowed, and their hooves thundered and boomed, kicking up giant clouds of dust.

Some festival-goers saw the stampede heading towards them. They pointed and screamed, running away in a terrified panic.

"Giddyup!" Axel yelled. "Faster, Hurricane! Fly like the wind!"

He gripped the saddle more tightly with his legs and felt Hurricane move up a gear. The gap was closing between them and the leading bull. Axel put all his trust in Hurricane. He pulled the rope off the saddle and slipped the coils into his right hand.

He whirled the lasso expertly round his head, as if he'd been doing it all his life. They were alongside now. Archie was wailing and his camera kept flashing in Axel's eyes.

Time seemed to slow down.

Axel saw a stall up ahead with a sign that read:

The terrified stallholder was frozen to the spot holding a glass of lemon crush in his hand. If Axel didn't do something now, it wasn't just the lemons that were going to get crushed...

The rope flew from his hands and the loop of the lasso circled the bull's head. Axel pulled back and tightened the rope. Then he wound the loose end round the pommel of his saddle and tied a quick knot.

Hurricane didn't want to get crushed like a lemon! But he knew what to do. As he reared up in the air, the rope tightened around the bull's neck, pulling it to the ground right in front of the lemon crush stall.

Axel spun round. The rest of the herd were nearly upon them. But now that their leader had stopped, they did too. The deafening stampede came to a halt as quickly as it had started. The cattle stood around looking confused, huffing and blowing as they got their breath back.

"Y-you saved my life!" Archie panted as he picked himself up from the dusty ground.

"It'll need saving again if you don't disappear before my uncle gets here!" Axel said crossly.

As Archie ran off to hide in the crowd, Axel noticed that the stallholder was still rooted to the spot. His shaking hand was making the ice tinkle in the glass of lemon crush that he was still holding.

"Erm – if you're not going to drink that," said Axel, "do you think I could have it? This is very thirsty work, you know!"

CHAPTER SIX

"Axel's gone and done it again!" Dad fumed.

They were sitting in the garden of their ranch. Newspapers and magazines were strewn across the table.

"Our concert only gets mentioned on the back page of the Red Rock newspaper, while Axel is spread all over the front!"

"Oh, Axel!" Mum sighed. "I don't know how you get yourself into these adventures. You could have hurt yourself really badly!"

Axel was sitting on the paddock fence. He scratched Hurricane between the ears. Uncle Ritchie had let Axel keep him.

"You wouldn't have let me fall off, would you, boy?" he asked his new best friend.

Hurricane tossed his flowing mane and whinnied his answer.

CELEBRITY GOSSIP MAGAZINE

RED ROCK RAMPAGE!

AXEL STORM saved the Red Rock Festival from being crushed under the hooves of hundreds of stampeding cattle yesterday.

"He was like a real rodeo star!" said Mr Lemon Squeezy, who came within seconds of certain death.

"AXEL SAVED MY LIFE TODAY!" he added.

Carmine Magenta, Mayor of Red Rock, awarded Axel the freedom of the valley. "Axel is a great example to the youth of today," she said.

Axel was unavailable for comment. His uncle said, "That boy sure has a way with horses!"

By ace reporter, Archie Flash.

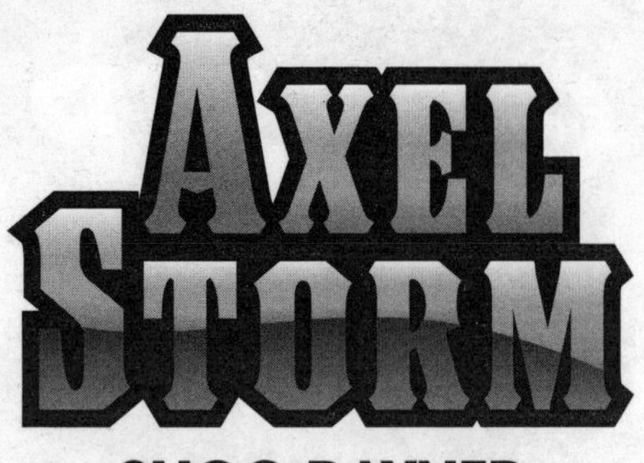

SHOO RAYNER

COLA POWER	978 1 40830 264 4
STORM RIDER	978 1 40830 265 1
JUNGLE FORTRESS	978 1 40830 266 8
DIAMOND MOON	978 1 40830 267 5
DEATH VALLEY	978 1 40830 268 2
SEA WOLF	978 1 40830 269 9
POLAR PERIL	978 1 40830 270 5
PIRATE CURSE	978 1 40830 271 2

ALL PRICED AT £3.99